But George did not like salad.

Can we help?

Yuck!

5

The Best Lunch

Adapted by
Katie Dale

Learn Phonics with Peppa Pig

Phonics teaches children to read by learning the sounds of a language. They start by learning the sound for each letter or combination of letters, which helps them to break down words into sounds (**th-i-nk**). They can then blend these sounds together to read whole words ("think"). This is called sounding out and blending.

As children learn more sounds, they will meet them in lots of different combinations. With practice, they will learn to sound out and blend the sounds together to read new words.

Listen carefully as your child reads the **Learn with Peppa** stories with you. Encourage them to sound out and blend each word. If they find a word difficult, help them to sound it out. Most importantly, have fun!

Tap your finger under each dot. Drag your finger along each line. Say each sound as you do so, and then blend the sounds together to read the whole word. Sometimes, two letters together can make one sound.

r   a   bb   i   t
·   ·   —   ·   ·

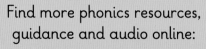

Find more phonics resources, guidance and audio online:

www.learnwithpeppa.com

The Best Lunch

Story warm-up

Read the sounds
Practise sounding out and blending to read these words.

a v oi d e d

c o ll e c t e d

c r o ss

f or k

f r e sh

m u n ch

p r e t e n d e d

p u dd i ng

s m e ll

Practise the words
These words cannot be sounded out in this way. Read them with your child.

all	are	do	full	he	like
me	no	of	said	so	the
they	was	we	when		

Meet the friends
These names are not as easy to sound out and blend! Read them with your child.

George   Granny Pig   Mummy Pig

3

Grandpa Pig collected stacks of crisp salad from his garden.

7

Granny Pig clapped her hands when she spotted the fresh food.

Granny Pig chopped the salad.

George did not like
the smell.

Grandpa Pig rang the bell for lunch.

Clink!
Clink!

George was cross. He clamped his lips shut as they all tucked in.

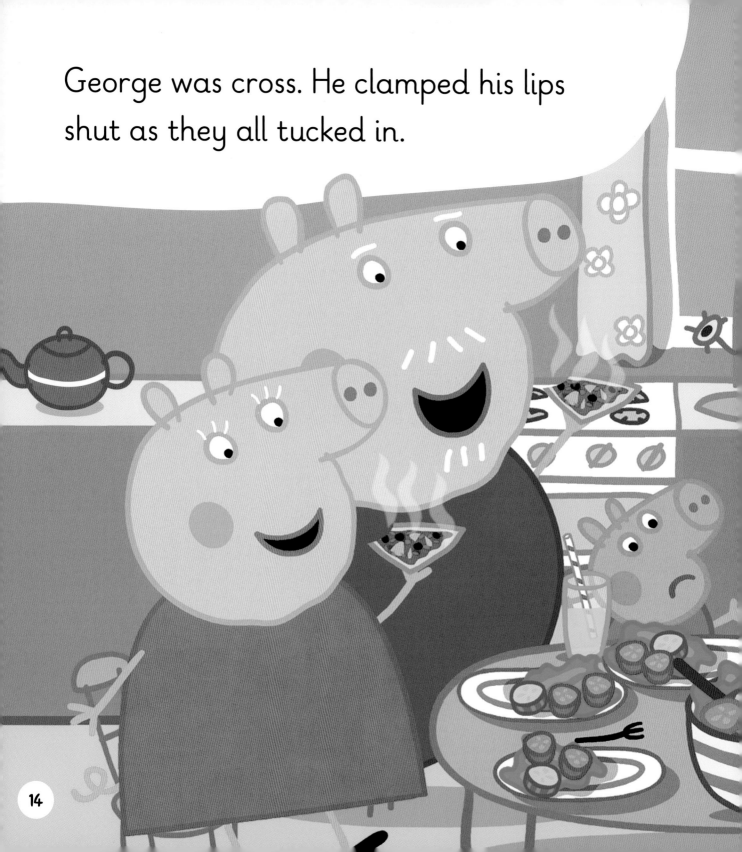

Mummy Pig said, "Trust me, you will like it!"

But George avoided her fork and pretended he was full.

Grunt!

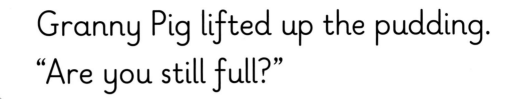

Granny Pig lifted up the pudding.
"Are you still full?"

No!

Granny Pig said, "Can you finish the salad, then?"

So George did just that.

Pudding was the best part of lunch!

Chomp!

Chomp!

Have fun with Peppa Pig

 A Who said it?

Trust me, you will like it!

Are you still full?

What do you prefer, George?

Can we help?

 B

How did Grandpa Pig let everyone know that lunch was ready?

C   What happens next in the story? Pick the correct answer for each picture.

Peppa took the salad to Grandpa Pig.

Peppa took the salad to Granny Pig.

George clapped his hands.

George was cross.

Grandpa Pig finished all the pudding.

George finished all of his lunch.

Answers at the back of the book

LADYBIRD BOOKS

UK | USA | Canada | Ireland | Australia | India | New Zealand | South Africa
Ladybird Books is part of the Penguin Random House group of companies
whose addresses can be found at global.penguinrandomhouse.com.
www.penguin.co.uk   www.puffin.co.uk   www.ladybird.co.uk

Penguin
Random House
UK

Adapted from:
Peppa Pig: Peppa's Lunch first published by Ladybird Books Ltd 2020
Learn with Peppa Pig edition published by Ladybird Books Ltd 2023
001
© 2023 ABD Ltd/Ent. One UK Ltd/Hasbro

Adapted by Katie Dale
Phonics consultant: Charlotte Raby

Licensed by

Printed in China

The authorized representative in the EEA is Penguin Random House Ireland,
Morrison Chambers, 32 Nassau Street, Dublin D02 YH68

A CIP catalogue record for this book is available from the British Library

ISBN: 978-0-241-57628-1

All correspondence to:
Ladybird Books, Penguin Random House Children's
One Embassy Gardens, 8 Viaduct Gardens, London SW11 7BW

MIX
Paper from
responsible sources
FSC® C018179

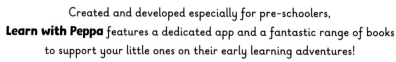

Created and developed especially for pre-schoolers,
Learn with Peppa features a dedicated app and a fantastic range of books
to support your little ones on their early learning adventures!

www.learnwithpeppa.com